PHILADELPHIA 76ERS

by Dave Jackson

Published by ABDO Publishing Company, 8000 West 78th Street, Edina, Minnesota 55439. Copyright © 2012 by Abdo Consulting Group, Inc. International copyrights reserved in all countries. No part of this book may be reproduced in any form without written permission from the publisher. SportsZone™ is a trademark and logo of ABDO Publishing Company.

Printed in the United States of America,
North Mankato, Minnesota
062011
092011

 THIS BOOK CONTAINS AT LEAST 10% RECYCLED MATERIALS.

Editor: Matt Tustison
Copy Editor: Nicholas Cafarelli
Series design: Christa Schneider
Cover production: Marie Tupy
Interior production: Carol Castro

Photo Credits: Matt Slocum/AP Images, cover, 47; Focus on Sport/Getty Images, 1, 9, 26, 31, 43 (top); NBAE/Getty Images, 4, 33; Bill Kostroun/AP Images, 7; AP Images, 11, 12, 17, 18, 21, 23, 25, 29, 37, 42, 43 (middle); Michael Okoniewski/AP Images, 15; Amy Sancetta/AP Images, 34; Jeff Mitchell/AP Images, 39, 43 (bottom); Kathy Kmonicek/AP Images, 41; Charlie Krupa/AP Images, 44

Library of Congress Cataloging-in-Publication Data
Jackson, Dave, 1970-
  Philadelphia 76ers / by Dave Jackson.
      p. cm. -- (Inside the NBA)
  Includes index.
  ISBN 978-1-61783-171-3
  1. Philadelphia 76ers (Basketball team)--History--Juvenile literature. I. Title.
  GV885.52.P45J34 2011
  796.323'640974811--dc23
                                    2011019408

TABLE OF CONTENTS

Chapter 1 .... "Fo, Fo, Fo," 4

Chapter 2 .... A Sport Picks Up Speed, 12

Chapter 3 .... Return of a Native, 18

Chapter 4 .... A Call to the Doctor, 26

Chapter 5 .... Search for an Answer, 34

Timeline, 42

Quick Stats, 44

Quotes and Anecdotes, 45

Glossary, 46

For More Information, 47

Index, 48

About the Author, 48

CHAPTER 1

"FO, FO, FO"

The Philadelphia 76ers always seemed to be just one player short. Despite having one of the best teams in the National Basketball Association (NBA) from 1976 to 1982, they had not won a league championship.

Three losses in the NBA Finals and another three losses in earlier playoff rounds had denied the club a title. The 76ers and their star, Julius Erving, desperately wanted a crown.

It was clear the player the team lacked was an imposing center. Philadelphia had Erving. He was a high-scoring forward with spectacular leaping ability and body control. The Sixers also had a steady point guard in Maurice Cheeks, a clutch shooter in Andrew Toney, and a tough defender in forward Bobby Jones. But Philadelphia never had an answer for opposing big men.

Center Moses Malone dribbles against the Lakers' Magic Johnson, *left*, and Kareem Abdul-Jabbar in the 1983 NBA Finals. Malone led the 76ers to a four-game sweep.

A BASKETBALL PIONEER

When Moses Malone debuted in the American Basketball Association (ABA) in 1974, he became the first player since 1963 to enter professional basketball directly from high school. The Petersburg, Virginia, native used his 6-foot-10, 260-pound body to become a superb scorer and rebounder.

Malone played 21 seasons—two in the ABA and 19 in the NBA—and scored more than 29,000 points in his professional career. Malone began his career with the ABA's Utah Stars in 1974–75.

Malone led the NBA in rebounding six times, including his first three seasons with the 76ers. His 16,212 rebounds ranked fifth in NBA history through the 2010–11 season. He also held one of the NBA's most impressive streaks. For 1,212 games in a row from 1978 to 1994, Malone played in the rugged world of the paint and never fouled out.

In 1977, the Sixers lost in the NBA Finals to the Portland Trail Blazers and their great center, Bill Walton. In 1980 and 1982, the Los Angeles Lakers and 7-foot-2 Kareem Abdul-Jabbar defeated the Sixers in the Finals. The 76ers also lost in seven games in the Eastern Conference finals in 1981 to the Boston Celtics. The Celtics featured big men Robert Parish and Kevin McHale.

Before the 1982–83 season, the Sixers got their man. They signed former Houston Rockets center Moses Malone. Malone was the league's Most Valuable Player (MVP) the previous season and helped the Rockets make the 1981 NBA Finals. At 6 feet 10 inches tall, Malone was shorter than some of the league's other top centers. But he was very strong.

The 76ers' Julius Erving, "Dr. J," rises for a shot against the Knicks during the 1983 Eastern Conference semifinals. Philadelphia swept the series in four games.

Malone delivered a great regular season. He averaged 24.5 points per game and led the league with 15.3 rebounds a contest. He was named the league's MVP for the second season in a row. The Sixers won 65 games and lost only 17 in the 1982–83 regular season. This gave them the NBA's best record. They were the favorites entering the playoffs.

Malone was asked his opinion of how the team would perform in the postseason. He was always a man who preferred actions to words. Malone said simply, "Fo, fo, fo." The comment was short for "four, four, four." This indicated that he thought the Sixers would win each of their series by winning the required four games. Even more, Malone was saying he expected each series to be a sweep.

It was a bold prediction. Few players had the confidence to predict a championship at the beginning of the playoffs. Even fewer would say their team could win every game.

Philadelphia opened the playoffs by sweeping the New York Knicks in four games. The 76ers thus earned a spot in the conference finals against the Milwaukee Bucks. The Sixers then won their first three meetings with the Bucks before Milwaukee won the fourth game. But the 76ers won the fifth game, 115–103, and took the series.

The Sixers were back in the Finals. And so were the Lakers. Los Angeles was missing forward James Worthy because of an injury. But the Lakers were still a dangerous team. They had Abdul-Jabbar, point guard Magic Johnson, and outside shooters Jamaal Wilkes and Norm Nixon.

The Lakers led at halftime of the first three games. But the

An American Original

Julius Erving was one of the best players in NBA history, and he might have been the very best player the ABA ever had. The ABA, a rival league to the NBA, existed from 1967 to 1976. Erving played in only five of the ABA's nine seasons. But he scored 11,662 points for the Virginia Squires and the New York Nets from 1971 to 1976 to rank fifth in league history. He was named the ABA's MVP three times and led the Nets to league championships in 1974 and 1976. He also thrilled crowds with countless slam dunks.

The 76ers' Moses Malone lets go of a free throw during the 1983 NBA Finals. Malone averaged 25.8 points and 18 rebounds in the series.

Sixers rallied to win the first two games in Philadelphia, 113–107 and 103–93. Then the 76ers came back from another halftime deficit and routed the Lakers 111–94 in Game 3 in Los Angeles. Nixon and forward Bob McAdoo were injured in that game. This left the already short-handed Lakers in even more trouble.

The Sixers were in command of the series. Erving was asked whether he would prefer that the team clinch the title in Philadelphia. Game 5 would be played there if the Lakers won Game 4. Erving craved

> ### Backcourt Partners
>
> Moses Malone and Julius Erving gained most of the fame on the 1982–83 team, but the Sixers' starting guards were also excellent players. Point guard Maurice Cheeks played 15 seasons and retired in the top 10 in NBA history in both assists and steals. Andrew Toney was a dangerous outside shooter who saved his best performances for the rival Boston Celtics. He scored 34 points to lead Philadelphia to a 120–106 upset win over host Boston in Game 7 of the 1982 Eastern Conference finals.

a championship after many years of falling short. He was not inclined to wait three extra days.

"That would mean 72 hours more of wondering," Erving said. "And I've wondered long enough."

But Los Angeles did not give up easily. The Lakers took another halftime lead and held a 93–82 advantage into the fourth quarter of Game 4. The Lakers still led 106–103 with 2:40 left. That is when Erving took over the game.

Following a Sixers free throw, Erving stole a pass from Abdul-Jabbar and coasted in for a dunk to tie the score. Johnson made a free throw for the Lakers. But the Sixers responded with a fast break that ended when Erving laid the ball into the basket and drew a foul. He then made the free throw. His three-point play gave the Sixers their first lead, at 109–107, since the first quarter.

After Abdul-Jabbar made a free throw, Erving shook off Johnson and buried a jump shot from the foul line. This gave Philadelphia a three-point lead. Dunks by Malone and Cheeks finished off the 115–108 win and the Sixers' first NBA championship in 16 years.

The Sixers did not quite live up to Malone's prediction.

Moses Malone, *right*, and Julius Erving celebrate while holding the title trophy after the 76ers won the 1983 NBA Finals. At left is league commissioner Larry O'Brien.

But they came very close by losing only once in 13 playoff games. For Erving, the victory in Los Angeles provided the ultimate Hollywood ending.

"Seven years is a long time," Erving said, referring to his last league championship, in the ABA with the New York Nets. "But it was well worth the wait."

Leader On and Off the Court

Billy Cunningham was a Hall of Fame forward for the 76ers over his nine seasons with the team in the 1960s and 1970s. Then he returned as Philadelphia's coach in 1977 and led the club for eight seasons. He won an NBA championship as a player on the 1966–67 team and as the coach of the 1982–83 team. He retired with the most wins of any coach in franchise history with 454.

CHAPTER 2
A SPORT PICKS UP SPEED

The NBA of today came about in 1949. Two rival leagues, the Basketball Association of America (BAA) and the National Basketball League (NBL), merged to form the new league.

The NBA had 17 teams for its first season in 1949–50. Six of those clubs had played in the NBL in the 1948–49 season. One of those teams was the Syracuse Nationals. The Nationals were originally a barnstorming squad called the Reds. Syracuse joined the NBL in 1946. It cost the club's owner, Danny Biasone, just $5,000 to enter the league.

When the NBL and the BAA merged, the Nationals—or Nats, as they were called—made a strong first impression. Syracuse finished the regular season 51–13 and reached

Al Cervi, shown in January 1950, was the coach and a guard for the NBA's Syracuse Nationals for parts of eight seasons. The Nats would later become the 76ers.

> ### The "L" before the "A"
>
> One of the two leagues that merged to form the NBA was the NBL. The NBL consisted of mostly Midwestern teams. Syracuse, located in the central part of New York state, represented the league's easternmost point. The league produced five teams that play in the current NBA: the Syracuse Nationals (now the 76ers), the Fort Wayne (now Detroit) Pistons, the Minneapolis (now Los Angeles) Lakers, the Rochester Royals (now the Sacramento Kings), and the Tri-Cities Blackhawks (now the Atlanta Hawks).

the inaugural NBA Finals in 1950. Forward Dolph Schayes and player-coach Al Cervi led the Nats. Syracuse faced the Minneapolis Lakers and their star center, George Mikan, in the Finals. The Lakers swept all three of their home games. This included a 110–95 victory in the clincher in Game 6.

The final score of that last contest was unusually high for the NBA. In those days, teams preferred to play a half-court game. Offenses were built around ball movement and patiently looking for the best shot. When the Lakers and the Nationals met again in the 1954 NBA Finals, neither team scored more than 87 points in a game. The highest point total came in Game 7. The host Lakers won the championship with an 87–80 victory in that contest.

Biasone felt games were played at too slow a pace. He suggested to NBA officials that the league needed a shot clock. This would shorten each team's possession and, Biasone believed, create a more exciting, high-scoring product. In 1954, the league adopted Biasone's proposal of a 24-second shot clock. Each team would now need to attempt a shot within the 24 seconds or lose possession of the ball. The shot clock's impact was immediate: Scoring

Danny Biasone, shown in 1992, proposed that the NBA use a 24-second shot clock, and the league adopted the rule in 1954. Biasone was the Nats' owner at the time.

in the league increased by more than 13 points per game in 1954–55.

With the Lakers' Mikan having retired, the Nationals tied for the best record in the league in 1954–55 at 43–29. Syracuse met the Fort Wayne Pistons in the NBA Finals.

The Nats won the first two games of the Finals at home. But

Why 24 Seconds?

Nationals owner Danny Biasone used simple math to determine the proper length of an NBA shot clock. He determined that in a well-paced game, each team attempted about 60 shots. So the total number of shots should be 120. In a 48-minute game, there were 2,880 seconds. Dividing 120 into 2,880 yields 24, and thus Biasone proposed a 24-second clock for teams to attempt a shot. The NBA adopted the shot clock and has retained it to this day.

A SPORT PICKS UP SPEED

the Pistons took the next three games on their floor. In Game 6, the host Nationals prevailed 109–104. In Game 7, visiting Fort Wayne jumped out to a 17-point advantage. It was at this point that Biasone's invention saved his team. Despite the lead, Fort Wayne could not simply hold the ball and run down the clock. The Pistons' shooting went cold. The Nats came back.

The score was tied 91–91 with 12 seconds remaining when the Pistons fouled the Nats' George King. He made one of two shots, putting his team ahead. Then he stole the ball from Fort Wayne to prevent the Pistons from taking the lead and dribbled out the clock. Syracuse won the NBA championship.

"I would have walked to California and back to give the Syracuse fans the title," Cervi, the team's coach, said afterward. In a small city like Syracuse, New York, the championship meant more than in larger cities.

Following their title, the Nationals continued to have a strong team led by Schayes. The forward averaged more than 20 points per game in six consecutive seasons starting in

Dolph and Danny

Dolph Schayes was without question the greatest player in Syracuse Nationals history. He joined the Nationals in 1949, for the team's first season in the NBA, out of New York University. The center played for the franchise until 1964, including its first season in Philadelphia. He averaged 18.5 points and 12.1 rebounds a game over his Hall of Fame career and made 12 All-Star teams—more than anyone in franchise history. In tribute to Nationals owner Danny Biasone, Schayes named his son Danny. Danny Schayes would star at Syracuse University and play 18 seasons in the NBA, from 1981 to 1999.

Nationals center Dolph Schayes had a reason to smile in January 1960 after he became the first NBA player to reach 15,000 career points.

1955–56. But the Nats could not get further than the Eastern Conference finals.

The Nationals made the playoffs every season after joining the NBA. But Syracuse proved to be too small a city to sustain a team in the league. In May 1963, Biasone sold the Nats to Irv Kosloff and Ike Richman. The team moved to Philadelphia. The club began play in the 1963–64 season in a new city with a new name—the Philadelphia 76ers.

A SPORT PICKS UP SPEED

CHAPTER 3

RETURN OF A NATIVE

When the Philadelphia 76ers made their debut in the fall of 1963, forward Dolph Schayes was near retirement and was serving as a player-coach.

The team had a new star in Hal Greer. Greer was a quick guard who had averaged nearly 20 points per game in the club's final season in Syracuse. Before their last season in Syracuse, the Nationals also had drafted forward Chet Walker out of Bradley University in Peoria, Illinois.

Greer and Walker were the first two important pieces of what would become one of the NBA's best teams. The most important piece came on January 15, 1965. That day, the Sixers traded three players and cash to the San Francisco Warriors for center Wilt Chamberlain.

Star center Wilt Chamberlain grabs a rebound over the Knicks' Walt Bellamy in March 1966. Chamberlain, a Philadelphia native, played with the 76ers from 1965 to 1968.

City of Hoops

When the Syracuse Nationals moved to Philadelphia, they came to a city with a long basketball tradition. During basketball's barnstorming days, the Philadelphia SPHAs were one of the best teams. SPHAs was an acronym for South Philadelphia Hebrew Association, the group that bought the players' uniforms. Many of the players were of Jewish heritage. The SPHAs' organizer and coach was Eddie Gottlieb. Gottlieb later coached and owned the NBA's Philadelphia Warriors, who won the 1956 NBA title and later featured legend Wilt Chamberlain. Gottlieb sold the Warriors in 1962, and they moved to San Francisco. But only one year later, Philadelphia got its new team, the 76ers.

Chamberlain, a native of Philadelphia, stood 7 feet 1. He had been the league's leading scorer for five consecutive years when he joined the 76ers. In one game in March 1962, he scored 100 points. This set a league record. He averaged a record 50.4 points per game in the 1961–62 season.

With Chamberlain averaging 30.1 points and 22.3 rebounds per game, the Sixers reached the playoffs in 1965. The 76ers beat the Cincinnati Royals in the first round. This put Philadelphia in the Eastern Division finals against the Boston Celtics and that team's own star center, Bill Russell.

During the first of what would be several big matchups between the teams, the series came down to a seventh game in Boston. With his team down 110–103, Chamberlain scored six consecutive points. Then he harassed Russell into a turnover on an inbounds pass.

With just five seconds left, the Sixers had a chance to win the game as Greer inbounded the ball. He tried to pass to Walker. But Boston's John Havlicek jumped and tipped the ball away. The Celtics' Sam Jones gathered the loose ball

The 76ers' Wilt Chamberlain, *right*, battles Celtics rival Bill Russell in the 1966 Eastern Division finals.

and dribbled out the remaining time. It was a heartbreaking loss for the Sixers.

The Celtics would go on to win the NBA title. The 76ers regrouped for another year. The 1964 NBA Draft had brought forward Luke Jackson of the University of Texas-Pan American. In 1965, the Sixers drafted Billy Cunningham, a forward, from the University

Battle of the Big Men

The rivalry between centers Wilt Chamberlain and Bill Russell actually began during Chamberlain's days with the Philadelphia Warriors. The Warriors and Russell's Boston Celtics met in the Eastern Division finals in 1960 and 1962, with the Celtics prevailing both times. After Chamberlain joined the 76ers in 1965, he met Russell and the Celtics in four consecutive division finals. The Celtics won three of those four, with the Sixers prevailing in 1967 on the way to their championship.

The first game demonstrated the teams' explosive offenses. The host Sixers prevailed 141–135 in overtime. Philadelphia took the second game 126–95. The Warriors bounced back at home and won the third game 130–124. The Sixers triumphed 122–108 in Game 4 and had a chance to clinch the championship on their home floor. However, Philadelphia lost 117–109 in Game 5.

It was back to San Francisco for Game 6. The Sixers led by one point in the closing seconds when Jackson won a critical jump ball. Walker grabbed the ball and hit two free throws to ice a 125–122 win that earned the team its first league championship since it had moved to Philadelphia.

The Sixers looked as if they might repeat in 1968. But they blew a three-games-to-one lead to Boston in the Eastern Division finals. They lost 100–96 in Game 7 at home. After the season, Hannum resigned as coach and Chamberlain was traded to the Los Angeles Lakers after the 76ers failed to agree on a new contract with him.

Cunningham, the team's new star, and Greer kept the Sixers competitive for a few seasons. But they never approached their great season of 1966–67. When Cunningham left for the rival ABA in 1972, everything fell apart. Six years after finishing with the best record in NBA history, the 76ers fell to 9–73. It was the worst record ever in the league.

76ers guard Hal Greer accepts a game ball from team owner Irv Kosloff after Greer passed the 20,000-point mark for his career in January 1971.

CHAPTER 4

A CALL TO THE DOCTOR

The Sixers turned the NBA's worst team ever, their 1972–73 squad, into a playoff team in just three years. And then, before the 1976–77 season, they added a true superstar. Julius Erving had led the New York Nets to two ABA titles. He became available when the ABA merged with the NBA and the Nets needed money to keep their franchise alive.

The Nets sold the 76ers the rights to Erving for $3 million. It was an investment that paid off. The forward gave the team a third scorer to go with forward George McGinnis and guard Doug Collins. And Erving's athletic ability made him an instant fan favorite in Philadelphia.

Erving was nicknamed "Dr. J" for his ability to "operate" on a basketball court. He had exceptional leaping ability. He also had large hands that allowed him to control the ball

The 76ers' Julius Erving soars for a dunk against the Knicks in the late 1970s. Erving's arrival in Philadelphia in 1976 gave the team a star it could build around.

FATHER OF THE DUNK

Julius Erving is often credited with making the slam dunk a popular element of basketball. His ability to fly through the air and finish at the basket led the ABA to introduce a Slam Dunk Contest.

The contest was held at halftime of the ABA's All-Star Game in Denver on January 27, 1976. Erving outdueled the Nuggets' David Thompson to win. Among other things, Erving launched himself from the foul line, 15 feet away from the basket, and slammed the ball into the hoop.

The NBA introduced its own Slam Dunk Contest during the All-Star Game weekend in 1984. Erving competed in the first event and made another dunk from the foul line. However, he missed one of his dunks and lost to the Phoenix Suns' Larry Nance. The contest was a hit, and it continues to be a part of the league's All-Star Game festivities.

while navigating his way to the basket.

Erving made an immediate impact on the Sixers. He led them in scoring in his first season. Erving and McGinnis averaged more than 21 points apiece, and Collins scored more than 18. The Sixers won 50 games in the regular season. In the postseason, they eliminated the defending NBA champion Boston Celtics in seven games. Philadelphia then beat the Houston Rockets in six games to reach the NBA Finals.

In the Finals, the Sixers met the Portland Trail Blazers. Portland was led by one of the game's top centers in Bill Walton and bruising forward Maurice Lucas. Philadelphia looked as if it would roll to the title after winning the series' first two games 107–101 and 107–89.

Philadelphia's Julius Erving goes up for a shot as Portland's Bill Walton, *left*, tries to block it in the 1977 NBA Finals. The 76ers lost in six games.

But the momentum changed in the second game. Sixers center Darryl Dawkins and Blazers forward Bob Gross crashed to the ground contesting a rebound. Players from both sides exchanged words and shoves. Lucas challenged Dawkins to a fight. The two players backed off. But Lucas had sent his message: The Blazers would fight to the end.

Back in Portland, the Blazers won Games 3 and 4 by a combined 54 points. Then they won Game 5 in Philadelphia 110–104 despite Erving's 37 points. The Sixers hung tough in Game 6 on the road. But Erving's 40 points were not enough.

> **Cast of Characters**
>
> Two of basketball's most memorable characters played on the Sixers' 1977 NBA runner-up team. Darryl Dawkins was a wide-bodied center who averaged 12 points per game over parts of 14 NBA seasons. But he was more famous for shattering glass backboards with his powerful dunks and for claiming to have been born on the imaginary planet Lovetron. Lloyd Free was a reserve guard who became one of the game's top scorers after the Sixers traded him before the 1978–79 season. His ability to score from anywhere on the court earned him the nickname "World," which he made his legal first name in 1981. He is still known as World B. Free.

McGinnis missed a jump shot in the closing seconds and Portland won 109–107 to claim the NBA championship.

The 76ers brought back a nearly identical team the next season and won 55 regular-season games. Early in the season, the Sixers fired coach Gene Shue and hired former star player Billy Cunningham to replace him. But again in the playoffs, a more physical team knocked out high-scoring Philadelphia. The Washington Bullets beat the Sixers in the Eastern Conference finals in six games.

The 76ers began reshaping their team following the playoff loss. Cunningham realized he needed better defenders. As a result, Philadelphia traded McGinnis to the Denver Nuggets for forward Bobby Jones. Also, the 76ers used a 1978 second-round draft pick on guard Maurice Cheeks from West Texas State University.

The 1978–79 season ended with the Sixers in the playoffs again. They rallied from a three-games-to-one deficit to force a seventh game in the Eastern Conference semifinals in San Antonio. But the host Spurs won 111–108 in the deciding game.

Left to right, 76ers defenders Julius Erving, Bobby Jones, and Maurice Cheeks surround the Lakers' Magic Johnson in the 1980 NBA Finals.

After the 1978–79 disappointment, the next season, the 76ers won 59 regular-season games. They then beat the 61-win Celtics, who were led by rookie forward Larry Bird, in five games in the conference finals. In the NBA Finals, Philadelphia and Los Angeles split the first four games. The Lakers won 108–103 in Game 5 at home. But they lost center Kareem Abdul-Jabbar to an ankle injury.

The Sixers planned to take advantage of Abdul-Jabbar's absence from the Lakers. But a Lakers rookie point guard

> ### A Rivalry Renewed
>
> In the 1960s, it was Wilt Chamberlain versus Bill Russell. In the 1980s, the Sixers-Celtics rivalry came back thanks to the respective talents of Julius Erving and Larry Bird. The two teams represented the Eastern Conference in every NBA Finals from 1980 to 1987. They met in the conference finals in 1980, 1981, 1982, and 1985, with each team winning twice. The rivalry was not limited to the playoffs. Erving and Bird got into an on-court fight during a regular-season game in Boston on November 9, 1984. Both were ejected from the game and fined $7,500.

finals en route to the NBA Finals. Meanwhile, the 62-win Sixers took a three-games-to-one lead in the Eastern Conference finals against the Celtics. But the Celtics won a pair of two-point games to force the series to a deciding seventh game in Boston.

The two teams battled to the end before Bird's jump shot with 1:03 left gave the Celtics a 91–89 lead. Boston ended up triumphing 91–90 to advance to the Finals, which the Celtics won.

History almost repeated itself in 1982. Again the Celtics and the 76ers met in the Eastern Conference finals. Again the Sixers took a three-games-to-one lead. And once more the Celtics took the next two games to force a seventh game in Boston.

The Sixers answered the challenge this time. Second-year named Earvin "Magic" Johnson, who was tall for his position at 6 feet 9, started at center in Game 6. Johnson scored 42 points as visiting Los Angeles won 123–107 to capture the title. The 76ers would have to wait another year for a shot at a championship.

It looked as if 1981 might be that year. The Rockets upset the defending champion Lakers in the Western Conference

76ers guard Andrew Toney drives against the Celtics' Charles Bradley in 1982. Toney had some of his best games against Boston, Philadelphia's biggest rival.

guard Andrew Toney had 34 points and Erving added 29 as the visiting Sixers won 120–106 to reach the Finals against the Lakers. Boston fans paid their conquerors the ultimate tribute, chanting "Beat LA!" as the final seconds ticked off.

It took the 76ers one more year before they could beat LA. The Lakers won the 1982 championship in six games. This prompted the Sixers to make the trade for Moses Malone. He teamed with Erving, Cheeks, Toney, Jones, and a group of role players. They led the Sixers to the NBA's best record in 1983 and their long-sought championship.

CHAPTER 5

SEARCH FOR AN ANSWER

After their 1983 championship, it took the Sixers 18 years to return to the NBA Finals.

They had some good teams throughout the 1980s. This was largely thanks to the 1984 first-round draft choice of forward Charles Barkley from Auburn University in Alabama.

Barkley combined with Julius Erving and Moses Malone to get Philadelphia to the 1985 Eastern Conference finals. But the Sixers lost to the Celtics in five games. Malone

Little Big Man

Charles Barkley left Auburn University with the nickname "The Round Mound of Rebound." He was listed at 6 feet 6 inches but was at least an inch shorter. But he used his 250-pound frame and great leaping ability to become one of the best rebounders in NBA history. He averaged 22.1 points and nearly 11.7 rebounds a game over his 16-year career. His first eight seasons came in Philadelphia, where he led the 76ers to six playoff appearances.

Philadelphia's Charles Barkley, *left*, leaps high to block a shot by Milwaukee's Alton Lister during a 1986 playoff game.

SEARCH FOR AN ANSWER

DRAFT-DAY DISASTER

In 1986, the Sixers won the NBA Draft's number one pick in the league's annual lottery.

But team owner Harold Katz, perhaps afraid to pay a large sum of money to a rookie, traded the pick to the Cleveland Cavaliers on the day before the draft. The Sixers received forward Roy Hinson in return. Then, on the same day, Katz traded center Moses Malone to the Washington Bullets, getting back forwards Jeff Ruland and Cliff Robinson.

Both trades proved to be a disaster for Philadelphia. Hinson, Ruland, and Robinson had all left the team by the time the 1989–90 season began. Malone played another six full seasons and parts of three more. And the number one pick that the Sixers gave up? The Cavaliers used it to pick center Brad Daugherty, who averaged 19 points per game and made five All-Star teams in eight seasons with Cleveland.

was traded before the 1986–87 season. Erving retired after that season. It was left to Barkley to lead the team in the years ahead.

The 76ers made three straight playoff appearances from 1989 to 1991. In the last two, Michael Jordan and the Chicago Bulls defeated the Sixers in five games. After Philadelphia failed to make the postseason in 1992, the team traded Barkley to the Phoenix Suns.

With Barkley gone, the Sixers tried four different coaches over the next five seasons. But they never won more than 26 games. After an 18–64 finish in 1995–96, the Sixers won the lottery for the first pick of the NBA Draft. They selected guard Allen Iverson from Georgetown University.

Iverson stood just 6 feet tall. But he was quick and

Guard Allen Iverson, *left*, and coach Larry Brown watch from the bench during a game in February 2000. The two were together with Philadelphia from 1997 to 2003.

fearless. When the Sixers hired veteran coach Larry Brown before the 1997–98 season, he and Iverson combined to instill a toughness in the team that had been lacking. In 1999, Philadelphia qualified for the playoffs for the first time in eight seasons. The Sixers upset the Orlando Magic in the first round but lost in the second round to the Indiana Pacers in four consecutive games.

The next season, the 76ers won 49 regular-season games. But the Pacers beat them again in the second round. This time, however, it took six games. The Sixers were improving.

In their two previous title seasons, the 76ers had gotten off to tremendous starts. In 1966–67, they began the season 46–4. In 1982–83, they started 50–7. So when the 2000–01 Sixers began the season with

SEARCH FOR AN ANSWER

10 straight wins, 76ers fans had dreams of another title.

Iverson was the team's only star. But he was almost all the Sixers needed. Iverson averaged a league-leading 31.1 points per game and won the MVP Award.

The 76ers, who played strong defense, cruised to the best record in the Eastern Conference. They finished 56–26. But things became more difficult in the playoffs. Philadelphia met old nemesis Indiana in the first round. The Sixers lost 79–78 in a sloppy Game 1. However, the Sixers rebounded to win the next three games to take the series.

In the second round, Philadelphia lost the series opener against the Toronto Raptors. The Sixers won three of the next four games. Iverson scored 54 points in Game 2 and 52 points in Game 5. But Toronto won the sixth game. In the deciding Game 7, the host Sixers survived 88–87.

Philadelphia's Eastern Conference finals opponent was the Milwaukee Bucks. The 76ers were concerned that Iverson was wearing out. He missed Game 3, which the Sixers lost. But Iverson delivered when the team needed him most. The series went to another Game 7. Iverson scored 44 points. Host Philadelphia pulled away to win 108–91.

A Crossover Star

Nicknamed "The Answer," guard Allen Iverson froze opposing defenders with his signature move, the crossover dribble. He would catch a defender leaning in one direction, then shift the ball across his body and move past the player in the other direction. This helped free him for open jump shots and drives to the lane, resulting in layups or fouls. Iverson led the 76ers in scoring in all 10 of his full seasons with the team. He led the NBA four times.

The 76ers' Allen Iverson goes up for a shot as the Lakers' Shaquille O'Neal tries to block it in Game 1 of the 2001 NBA Finals.

Again, the Sixers would play the Los Angeles Lakers in the Finals. And these Lakers, led by center Shaquille O'Neal and guard Kobe Bryant, looked unbeatable. They had won all 11 of their games that postseason and threatened to break the Sixers' 1982–83 record of only one playoff loss.

But the visiting Sixers put an end to the Lakers' streak in a surprising 107–101 overtime victory in Game 1. Iverson scored 48 points, prompting O'Neal to say, "Now, it's a series."

The underdog Sixers had the Lakers' attention. Los Angeles got back to business. Philadelphia stayed close in the next two games but lost both. Then the Lakers won Games 4 and 5 by double digits. The 76ers had fought. But in the end, the Lakers had more talent.

The 2001 trip to the NBA Finals was the Sixers' last for the decade. They made the playoffs six more times through the 2010–11 season but won only one series, in 2002–03. Brown resigned as coach after that season. Meanwhile, Iverson's aggressive style of play left him prone to injuries. He was traded to the Denver Nuggets in December 2006.

The 76ers finished 40–42 and 41–41, respectively, in the 2007–08 and 2008–09 seasons. They lost in the first round of the playoffs both times. During 2008–09, the team fired Maurice Cheeks, the former Philadelphia star guard, as coach. He had been hired before the 2005–06 season.

Philadelphia finished with a 27–55 record in 2009–10. But things were starting to look better for 2010–11. The Sixers had a new coach in Doug Collins. Like Cheeks, Collins was a former Sixers guard. Philadelphia had selected the 6-foot-6 Iguodala, a former University of Arizona standout, in the first round of the 2004 NBA Draft. He quickly developed into a reliable scorer who thrilled fans with his acrobatic dunks.

Iguodala and forward Elton Brand helped lead the way as two established players. The 76ers had plenty of promising youngsters as well. Guards Jrue Holiday and Louis Williams and forward Thaddeus Young showed signs that they were developing into solid pros. The team also had 6-foot-7 guard Evan Turner. The Sixers chose him second overall in the 2010 NBA Draft. Philadelphia hoped that, in time, Turner could develop into a star.

Sixers guard Andre Iguodala drives to the basket in February 2011. He was a steady standout even when the team struggled.

The young Sixers team finished 41–41 to qualify for the playoffs in 2010–11. However, the powerful Miami Heat awaited. The 76ers avoided getting swept by scraping out an 86–82 win at home in Game 4. However, the Heat closed it out with a 97–91 win in Game 5.

Philadelphia lost in the first round for the fourth time in four postseasons, but the young squad showed promise. Veteran Brand led the team, averaging 15.6 points per game in all five games. But Holiday was a close second averaging 14.2 points per game. Behind Iguodala and young players such as Turner and Holiday, the 76ers continue to give a city with a passion for basketball hope for another title soon.

TIMELINE

1946 — After seven years as the barnstorming Syracuse Reds, the Syracuse Nationals join the NBL.

1949 — The NBL merges with the BAA to form the NBA. The Nats are one of six NBL teams to enter the new league.

1950 — The Nationals finish the 1949–50 season 51–13. Syracuse qualifies for the first NBA Finals but loses in six games to the George Mikan-led Minneapolis Lakers.

1955 — One year after finishing as runners-up to the Lakers again, the Nationals, with the help of star forward Dolph Schayes, win their first NBA championship. On April 10, the Nats outlast the visiting Fort Wayne Pistons 92–91 in Game 7 of the NBA Finals to clinch the title.

1963 — Danny Biasone sells the Nats to Ike Richman and Irv Kosloff, who move the team to Philadelphia and rename it the 76ers. The 76ers begin play in the 1963–64 season.

1967 — Led by Wilt Chamberlain, the Sixers finish 68–13 for the NBA's best regular-season record ever at the time. Philadelphia advances to the NBA Finals and beats San Francisco in six games for the crown. After the season, the 76ers move to their new home arena, The Spectrum.

1976 — The Sixers return to the playoffs behind former ABA standout forward George McGinnis. Following the season, Philadelphia signs another former ABA star in forward Julius Erving.

1977 — In his first NBA season, Erving leads the 76ers to a 50–32 record and a trip to the NBA Finals. Philadelphia takes a two-games-to-none lead over the Portland Trail Blazers but loses the final four games and the series.

1980	The 76ers return to the NBA Finals but fall in six games to the Los Angeles Lakers.
1982	After a dramatic seven-game victory in the Eastern Conference finals over the Boston Celtics, the Sixers again lose to the Lakers in six games in the NBA Finals.
1983	After signing star center Moses Malone, Philadelphia coasts to an NBA-best 65–17 record in the 1982–83 regular season. In the playoffs, the 76ers win 12 of their 13 games and sweep the Lakers in the NBA Finals.
1984	The New Jersey Nets upset the defending champion 76ers in the first round of the playoffs in April. On June 19, Philadelphia selects Auburn University forward Charles Barkley with the fifth overall pick in the NBA Draft. Barkley would lead the Sixers to the playoffs six times in his eight seasons with the team.
1996	With the top pick in the NBA Draft on June 26, the 76ers select Georgetown University guard Allen Iverson. Iverson would play 11 seasons for the team, leading the NBA in scoring four times. The Sixers move into the brand-new CoreStates Center for the 1996–97 season.
2001	Iverson wins the NBA's MVP Award and leads the 76ers past the Indiana Pacers, the Toronto Raptors, and the Milwaukee Bucks in the playoffs. In the NBA Finals, Philadelphia falls in five games to Los Angeles.
2010	After finishing 27–55 in the 2009–10 season, the 76ers select Ohio State University guard Evan Turner with the second overall pick in the NBA Draft on June 24. The Sixers hoped that Turner and other young players such as guard Jrue Holiday and forward Thaddeus Young could help lead the team back to prominence.

QUICK STATS

FRANCHISE HISTORY
Syracuse Nationals (1949–63)
Philadelphia 76ers (1963–)

NBA FINALS
(wins in bold)

1950, 1954, **1955**, **1967**, 1977, 1980, 1982, **1983**, 2001

CONFERENCE FINALS
1967, 1977, 1978, 1980, 1981, 1982, 1983, 1985, 2001

KEY PLAYERS
(position[s]; years with team)

Charles Barkley (F; 1984–92)
Wilt Chamberlain (C; 1964–68)
Maurice Cheeks (G; 1978–89)
Doug Collins (G; 1973–81)
Billy Cunningham (F; 1965–72, 1974–76)
Julius Erving (F; 1976–87)
Hal Greer (G/F; 1958–73)
Allen Iverson (G; 1996–2006, 2009–10)
Bobby Jones (F; 1978–86)
Moses Malone (C/F; 1982–86, 1993–94)
Dolph Schayes (F; 1949–64)
Andrew Toney (G; 1980–88)

KEY COACHES
Al Cervi (1949–56):
  294–201; 34–26 (postseason)
Billy Cunningham (1977–85):
  454–196; 66–39 (postseason)
Alex Hannum (1960–63, 1966–68):
  257–145; 26–20 (postseason)

HOME ARENAS
State Fair Coliseum (1949–51)
Onondaga County War Memorial (1951–63)
Convention Hall and Philadelphia Arena (1963–1967)
The Spectrum (1967–1996)
Wells Fargo Center (1996–)
  Also known as CoreStates Center, First Union Center, and Wachovia Center

* All statistics through 2010–11 season

QUOTES AND ANECDOTES

The 1954–55 Syracuse Nationals achieved an important milestone. Nats forwards Earl Lloyd and Jim Tucker became the first two African-American players to win an NBA championship. Lloyd played in all 72 games for the Nats, averaging 10.2 points per game.

Hall of Fame center Wilt Chamberlain scored 50 points in a game 11 times for the 76ers. He also scored 50 points in a game 11 times against the franchise, as a member of the Philadelphia/San Francisco Warriors. Nine of those 11 performances came against the Syracuse Nationals, before the franchise moved to Philadelphia and became the 76ers.

Willie Burton, a 6-foot-8 forward, played in only 316 games in the NBA, but he had his most memorable game with the Sixers. Released earlier in the 1994–95 season by the Heat, Burton gained some revenge by scoring 53 points against Miami in a 105–90 Philadelphia win on December 13, 1994. He set a Spectrum scoring record, topping the 52 points scored by the Chicago Bulls' Michael Jordan in 1988. "I'm going to have a hard time sleeping tonight," Burton said. "I just want to savor this."

The 76ers have hired several of their former players as coaches. Billy Cunningham won an NBA championship as both a Sixers player, in 1967, and a coach, in 1983. Philadelphia's coach as of 2011, Doug Collins, was also one of only two players the Sixers had taken number one overall in the NBA Draft. Allen Iverson was the other, in 1996. Philadelphia selected Collins first overall in 1973. Other former Sixers who later coached the team were Dolph Schayes, Matt Guokas, Fred Carter, and Maurice Cheeks.

GLOSSARY

acronym

A name formed by taking the first letter or letters of each word in a phrase.

barnstorming

Traveling from place to place to play.

contract

A binding agreement about, for example, years of commitment by a basketball player in exchange for a given salary.

debut

A first appearance.

distinction

Something for which a person or team is known or recognized.

franchise

An entire sports organization, including the players, coaches, and staff.

harassed

Bothered or annoyed.

inaugural

The first time something occurs.

instill

To build a quality in a team.

nemesis

A strong, frequent opponent.

playoffs

A series of games in which the winners advance in a quest to win a championship.

rival

An opponent that brings out great emotion in a team, its fans, and its players.

signature

Uniquely a characteristic of a particular person.

trade

A move in which a player or players are sent from one team to another.

FOR MORE INFORMATION

Further Reading

Karabell, Eric. *The Best Philadelphia Sports Arguments*. Naperville, IL: Sourcebooks, Inc., 2008.

Lynch, Wayne. *Season of the 76ers*. New York: St. Martin's Press, 2002.

Mallozzi, Vincent, with Dave Anderson. *Doc: The Rise and Rise of Julius Erving*. Hoboken, NJ. Wiley & Sons, 2009.

Web Links

To learn more about the Philadelphia 76ers, visit ABDO Publishing Company online at **www.abdopublishing.com**. Web sites about the 76ers are featured on our Book Links page. These links are routinely monitored and updated to provide the most current information available.

Places to Visit

Naismith Memorial Basketball Hall of Fame
1000 West Columbus Avenue
Springfield, MA 01105
413-781-6500
www.hoophall.com
This hall of fame and museum highlights the greatest players and moments in the history of basketball. Wilt Chamberlain and Julius Erving are among the former 76ers enshrined here.

The Palestra
220 South 32nd Street
Philadelphia, PA 19104
215-898-6151
www.philadelphiabig5.org/palestra
The home arena of the University of Pennsylvania basketball teams was opened in 1927 and includes a museum about the city of Philadelphia's rich basketball history.

Wells Fargo Center
3601 South Broad Street
Philadelphia, PA 19148
800-298-4200
www.wellsfargocenterphilly.com
This has been the 76ers' home arena since 1996.

INDEX

American Basketball Association (ABA), 6, 8, 11, 24, 27, 28

Barkley, Charles, 35–36
Basketball Association of America (BAA), 13
Biasone, Danny (owner), 13, 14, 15, 16, 17
Boston Celtics, 6, 10, 20–22, 24, 28, 31–33, 35
Brand, Elton, 40–41
Brown, Larry (coach), 37, 40

Cervi, Al (player and coach), 14, 16
Chamberlain, Wilt, 19–24, 32
Cheeks, Maurice (player and coach), 5, 10, 30, 33, 40
Collins, Doug (player and coach), 27–28, 40
Cunningham, Billy (player and coach), 11, 21–22, 24, 30

Dawkins, Darryl, 29–30

Erving, Julius "Dr. J," 5, 8, 9–11, 27–29, 33, 35–36

Fort Wayne Pistons, 14, 15–16
Free, Lloyd "World" B., 30

Greer, Hal, 19, 20, 22, 24

Hannum, Alex (coach), 22, 24
Hinson, Roy, 36
Holiday, Jrue, 40–41
Houston Rockets, 6, 28, 32

Iguodala, Andre, 40–41
Iverson, Allen, 36–38, 40

Jackson, Luke, 21–22, 24
Jones, Bobby, 5, 22, 30, 33
Jones, Wali, 22

Katz, Harold (owner), 36
King, George, 16
Kosloff, Irv (owner), 17

Los Angeles Lakers, 6, 8–10, 14, 24, 31–32, 33, 39–40

Malone, Moses, 6–8, 10, 33, 35, 36
McGinnis, George, 27–28, 30

National Basketball League (NBL), 13, 14
NBA Finals
  1950, 14
  1954, 14
  1955, 15
  1967, 23–24

  1977, 6, 28, 30
  1980, 6, 31–32,
  1982, 6, 33
  1983, 8–10, 33, 35
  2001, 39–40
New York Nets, 8, 11, 27

Philadelphia Warriors, 20–22
Portland Trail Blazers, 6, 28–30

Richman, Ike (owner), 17
Robinson, Cliff, 36
Ruland, Jeff, 36

San Francisco Warriors, 19, 20, 22, 23, 24
Schayes, Danny, 16
Schayes, Dolph (player and coach), 14, 16, 19
Shue, Gene (coach), 30
Syracuse Nationals, 13, 14–17, 19, 20

Toney, Andrew, 5, 10, 33
Turner, Evan, 40

Walker, Chet, 19, 20, 22, 24
Williams, Louis, 40

Young, Thaddeus, 40

About the Author

Dave Jackson is a freelance writer and former sportswriter with the *Star Tribune* and the Associated Press in Minneapolis, Minnesota. Since 1997, he has worked in corporate communications, helping large companies improve their communications with key stakeholders. He and his wife live in Dallas, Texas.

JAN / 2012

3 1799 00433 6707

REMOVED FROM COLLECTION

WEST ISLIP PUBLIC LIBRARY
3 HIGBIE LANE
WEST ISLIP, NEW YORK 11795

4/13-0 9/4.2

DEMCO